My Brother Is from Outer Space

(The Book of Proof)

VIVIAN OSTROW

Illustrations by

ERIC BRACE

ALBERT WHITMAN & COMPANY

Morton Grove, Illinois

This book is dedicated to my family: Larry, Alex, and William.

You're out of this world! V.O.

To my parents, Joyce and Virg, who raised me as though

I was from this planet. E.B.

Library of Congress Cataloging-in-Publication Data

Ostrow, Vivian.
My brother is from outer space / Vivian Ostrow; illustrations by Eric Brace.
p.   cm.
Summary: Alex compares his younger brother William with himself and concludes that because
William is so different, he must have come from outer space to join this otherwise perfect family.
ISBN 0-8075-5325-5
[1. Brothers—Fiction.   2. Sibling rivalry—Fiction.] I. Brace, Eric, ill.   II. Title.
PZ7.O855My   1996   95-38321
[E]—dc20   CIP   AC

Design by Susan B. Cohn.
The text of this book is set in Lemonade Bold.
The illustrations are rendered in acrylics, photo collage, and a dab of colored pencil for good measure.

I know brothers are supposed to be different. (Otherwise parents would have it too easy.) But not <u>this</u> different. It's impossible! There is only one explanation . . .

MY BROTHER IS FROM OUTER SPACE
(and this book has the proof).

Wait. I must be confusing you.
Let me start at the beginning . . .

Long, long ago, when my mom and dad were young(?), they met, fell in love, and got married.

A few years later, they got lonely (I guess), so they had a baby. That's me, Alex.

WE WERE THE PERFECT FAMILY.

More years passed, and for no reason I can think of, they had another baby. They named him William.

I'm sure William was born a human baby. But during his first night at the hospital odd things happened. There was a terrible storm with flashing lights and strange noises. In all the confusion, no one noticed evil aliens take my real brother and leave this "thing" in his place. I don't know why they did it, but I do know LIFE WAS NEVER THE SAME AT OUR HOUSE.

Lots of people said William was cute and that he looked like me. No way! Look closely. Can you see the big difference?

My mouth is closed, and William's mouth is open.

Baby Alex   Baby William

Whether he was crying or screaming or eating or sleeping, William's mouth was ALWAYS open. I'm sure that on William's world, they breathe through their mouths. Imagine a whole planet of beings who can't keep their mouths shut!

Before William could talk, he babbled. He got very mad when we didn't understand him. After weeks of thinking about it, I finally figured out what his favorite sentence meant.

* I am Gub from the Planet Dinkville. You must obey me.

I am smarter than you.

Even when William grew out of his babbling baby stage, he made no sense. Mom said I didn't understand him because we were as different as day and night.

Sometimes I felt Mom knew more about "Weird William" than she was saying. I guess it's not easy to admit your son is from Planet Who-Knows-Where.

One day I couldn't take it any longer. I told my parents the awful truth. They laughed and brought out the family photo album.

Staring at me were a very odd bunch with funny faces, strange clothes, and goofy hair.

Dad said, "Even in the same family, people can look—and be—very different." He compared Great-Great-Grandpa Wolf's nose with his own.

He also explained that behavior like
shyness and goofiness might run in families.
Grandma Esther was always making jokes.
Great-Uncle Jake had a fingernail collection.

Cousin Leo acted as if he were king of the family. And Great-Aunt Sura was a wild dresser though she was very quiet.

Dad's message was clear: William was normal (for our family).

William <u>normal</u>? No way! He wasn't even <u>human</u>!

I would make my own album. I'd collect facts, gather clues, and find answers.

I'd put it all together and make "The Book of Proof."

First, the hard facts:

NOT WANTED

Brother from Outer Space

NAME: Gub   ALIAS: William

BIRTHPLACE: The planet Dinkville.

DESCRIPTION: Alien disguised as human.

AGE: 8 going on 800.

HEIGHT: Tall (in a short family).

WEIGHT: Thin (although he eats all the time).

FINGERPRINTS: (Notice anything odd?)

HAIR: Dirty blond, straight, always neat but never combed.

EYES: Brown, possible X-ray vision.

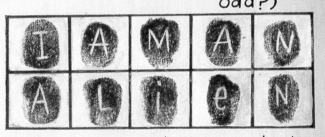

LAST SEEN: Wearing jeans and a striped green shirt.

SCARS: Not yet, but I don't know how much longer I can control myself.

MASTER PLAN: To wreck my life and take over the world.

CAUTION: He looks human and appears friendly, but he is armed: with a large open mouth, tricks up his sleeve, and superpowers.

As my "Weird William" research continued, I found clues everywhere.

TALKING: I talked only when I had something to say. William talked ALL the time (even in his sleep). The phone was his favorite toy. I wonder if he could call Dinkville from our house?

Hz, Nyb. Xʈ'w ue, Gyb.*

*Hi, Nub. It's me, Gub.

*Hi, Gub. I miss you. Send pizza.

WiLLiAM'S RePORt CaRd

SUBJECT	FINALS	GRADES	COMMENTS
Science	60	95	A GENIUS
English	68	92	"Great Kid"
Social Studies	79	91	"I love him"
Math	80	100	"WOW!!"
GENERAL COMMENTS			Great Student

THiS iSn't Fair!

LEARNING: William rarely got punished in school although his favorite subject was clowning around. Most of William's teachers retired after having him in their classes.

In spite of always fooling around and never studying, William got good marks. I guess aliens have the power to make teachers (and parents) see what they want them to see!

SLEEPING: I sleep with my head on the pillow and my body under the covers. I wake up in the same position I fall asleep in.

William sleeps like a wild man. He tosses, talks, and makes odd noises. His blankets always land in a ball on the floor. Sometimes he winds up on the floor, too.

William tries to copy human sleep behavior, but he gets it all wrong.

PLAYING: William thought he was a champ in everything, but his favorite sport was basketball. After weeks of hearing about what a great player he was, I decided to see for myself. To my surprise, he was fantastic! When he jumped, his feet seemed to have wings. His shots landed in the basket every time. I shouldn't have been too surprised that William played as though he had superhuman powers. He did.

When I put all the facts together, they added up to this: the aliens made William look human ... but they couldn't fool me.

I could see beneath the surface to the ugly truth.

Once, William slipped up. It was dinnertime, and he had just finished eating. He stood, and in a soft, clear voice he said . . .

AMAZING! Proof positive that William was an alien. Would Dad call 911 or the FBI? Neither! He just kept on eating!

Mom, however, had heard the whole thing. Good old Mom! And she reacted immediately—by laughing so hard she cried.

IT WAS HOPELESS. I realized I would have to hide *my* book (for now).

Someday, when William had either revealed his alien self, gone back to his home planet, or taken over the universe, I would bring out my book.

The world would finally know "the awful truth," and everyone would see that I knew it all along.

My book stayed hidden for a long time.
Then one day when William was helping me
pack for college, he discovered it. Before
I could grab the book, William started
reading it. He laughed his head off (aliens
can do that).

After William pulled himself together, he
said a very weird thing . . .

As William slowly walked out of my
room, he giggled that goofy giggle of his.

Those aliens have an answer
for everything!